The Gift Box

Rohan Henry

Abrams Books for Young Readers
New York

The illustrations in this book were made with
pen and ink and watercolor on paper.

Cataloging-in-Publication Data has been applied for
and may be obtained from the Library of Congress.
ISBN: 978-1-4197-0167-2

Text and illustrations copyright © 2012 Rohan Henry

Book design by Rohan Henry and Meagan Bennett

Printed and bound in China
10 9 8 7 6 5 4 3 2 1

Abrams Books for Young Readers are available at special discounts when
purchased in quantity for premiums and promotions as well as fundraising
or educational use. Special editions can also be created to specification.
For details, contact specialsales@abramsbooks.com or the address below.

ABRAMS
THE ART OF BOOKS SINCE 1949
115 West 18th Street
New York, NY 10011
www.abramsbooks.com

To Lynette and Albert Beckford

"Ollie, you should have finished cleaning up your toys by now," said Mama Elephant.

"I helped Kitty put away her toys first," said Ollie.

Mama laughed.

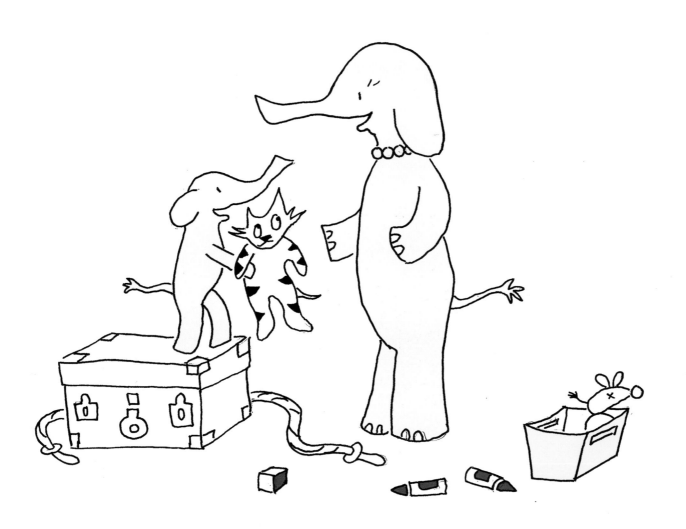

Mama Elephant scooped Ollie up,
swung him through the air,
and kissed him on the cheek.

"You are a beautiful gift," she told him.

"I'm a beautiful gift," sang Ollie.

Then he ran off to
find his best friend,
Benjamin.

"I'm a wonderful, delightfully marvelous, incredibly beautiful gift!"

Ollie skipped, danced, jumped, and leaped higher than he ever had as he hurried along.

"Guess what I am,"
Ollie asked his friend.

"That's easy," replied Benjamin.
"You're my best friend."

"No," said Ollie, "guess again."

Then he ran around in a circle so
Benjamin could get a look from all sides.

"You're a quick friend?"
said Benjamin.

"No, that's not it,"
said Ollie.

"I'll give you
one last clue,
Benjamin."

Ollie fetched a gift
box and some ribbon.

He wrapped himself
in the ribbon . . .

. . . and climbed into
the box.

"Ta-da!" Ollie said as
he popped up.

"Ribbon . . . gift box . . . You MUST
be a BEAUTIFUL friend!"

"WRONG," scolded Ollie.
Why couldn't Benjamin guess?
"Look closer!"

"I know exactly
what you are . . .

. . . a CLOSE friend,"
whispered Benjamin.

"I give up," sighed Ollie. Then he sank down into the gift box and wished he could just disappear.

"May I play with your balloon?" asked Benjamin.

"NO, YOU MAY NOT!" yelled Ollie.

"May I borrow some ribbon?" asked Benjamin.

"NO, YOU MAY NOT!" yelled Ollie.

"Well, may I climb into your gift box and sit next to you?" asked Benjamin.

"NEVER!"

screamed Ollie.

Ollie saw how his words
hurt Benjamin.

"I didn't mean that," Ollie said.
"I'm sorry."

"Of course you may play with my balloon if you want to. Here, have some ribbon."

"May I sit next to you?" asked Benjamin.

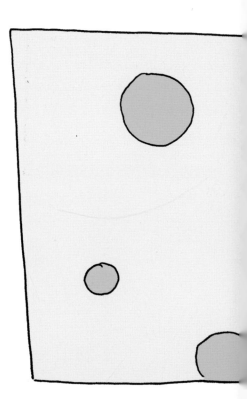

"Of course," replied Ollie.

"I knew you'd invite me
in sooner or later,"
said Benjamin.

"You know me so well,"
Ollie said.

Ollie and Benjamin
played all day long.
They played pirate ship . . .

. . . railroad
yard . . .

. . . and secret
hideout cave,
until it was
time for Ollie
to head home.

"Guess what I am!" Benjamin asked his friend.

"My best friend with dog breath carrying a gift box?" asked Ollie.

"Nope, guess again!"